First Published 2024
Text copyright © Taylor Hassel
Illustrations copyright © Taylor Hassel

ISBN 9798218383244

For our girls, we love you more than you will ever know.
-Mom & Dad

To my girlfriend and family, thank you for everything. Love you very much.
-O.T.

"Good morning, Little Ducks,
the sun's about to rise.
A day of adventures awaits,
let's eat breakfast; a sweet surprise."

"I want a bowl of porridge, please," Sister Duck softly quacks.

"Remember Little Duck,
don't yuck someone's yum.
Let's be kind and not dismiss.
We don't say 'ew'
to someone else's bliss.

Now heading to the shops,
they waddle down the street.

They spot their neighbor, Mrs. Whiskers.
She's selling a delightful treat.

Wading home through the lake, they float past a field.

When they spot a group of little pigs.
"Would you like to play with us?"
the big one squealed.

"Remember Little Duck,
don't yuck someone's yum.
Welcome new friends when they want to play.
And you might end up having a really good day."

Back inside with Sister Duck, it's time to play together. "This game is lame!" he shouts with a ruffle of his feathers.

The cards take flight and scatter wide while tears fill her eyes.

"It doesn't matter what others eat or drink or the colors of their vests.

Don’t yuck
someone’s yum.”

Made in United States
Troutdale, OR
05/08/2024

19749709R00029